Farmer George
and the Snowstorm

Other books in the series:

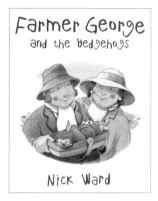

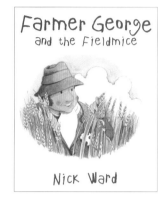

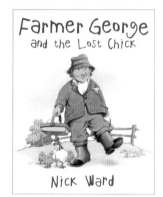

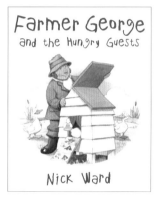

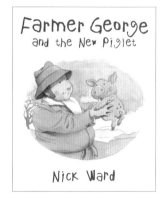

Farmer George
and the Snowstorm

NICK WARD

CHRYSALIS CHILDREN'S BOOKS

For Jo and Mathew

A PAVILION CHILDREN'S BOOK

First published in 2001

This paperback edition first published in Great Britain in 2003 by
Chrysalis Children's Books
64 Brewery Road
London N7 9NT
www.chrysalisbooks.co.uk

Designed by Ness Wood at Zoom Design
Cover design by Keren-Orr Greenfeld

A CIP catalogue record for this book is available from the British Library

ISBN 1 84365 021 5

Set in Bell MT
Printed and bound in Singapore by Kyodo
Colour Origination in Hong Kong by AGP Repro (HK) Ltd

2 4 6 8 10 9 7 5 3 1

This book can be ordered direct from the publisher. Please contact the Marketing Department.
But try your bookshop first.

Early one winter evening, Farmer
George looked out of his window.
Large flakes of snow filled the air.
A strong wind picked them up,
buffeting them against the window.

"I'd better go and check the animals,"
said Farmer George to Dotty, his wife.
"Wear those nice mittens I knitted
you," she said. "It's bitter out there."

Farmer George put on his thick winter coat and his nice new mittens, and stepped out into the yard. Crunch! His boots sank into the crisp white snow. "Ooh, it's cold," he gasped. "Come on, Tam. Let's go!"

Farmer George had just checked that all the animals in the yard were safe when he heard a noise coming from the top field. "Baa! BAA!"
"Oh dear," said Farmer George. "The sheep won't have any food. Their grass will be covered with snow!"

Farmer George got a bale of straw
from his barn and climbed on to his
tractor. But the tractor wouldn't start.
"Oh no!" thought Farmer George.
"What shall I do now?"

"There will be extra sugar lumps for you tonight, Sidney," said George, as they marched through the driving snow. "Good lad!"
When they reached the top field, the sheep were panicky. "Help!" they bleated. "Quick!"

Farmer George lifted the straw into their cosy hut. "Here you are," he said. But that wasn't the problem after all.

"It's Larry," they cried. "He's stuck!"
"Where?" asked George.
"Outside, in the ditch. Quick!"

Larry had sunk deep into a snowdrift and couldn't get out.

"Oh dear," muttered Farmer George. Holding on to Sidney's reins he managed to reach down and pull Larry out.

"He's very cold and hungry,"
said George.
"Let's get him back to the farm."

All night long, hour after hour, George
and Dotty held Larry in their arms.
They rubbed him to warm him up, and
tried to feed him from a bottle of milk.

"Will he be all right?" asked Dotty.
"I hope so," sighed George.
"We'll have to wait and see."
Eventually, they both
dozed off...

"Baa!"
George and Dotty woke with a start!
Larry was trotting round the parlour,
happy and well.
"Hooray!"

All the farm animals came to see
how Larry was.
"Larry's fine," George told Woolly, his
mother. "We'll just keep an eye on him
for one more day."

Which left the rest of the day for the animals to enjoy the snow…

…and for Sidney to enjoy his extra sugar lumps!

"Thank you, Sidney."

Some of Farmer George's animals have been playing in the snow. Can you tell which footprints belong to which animal?

More titles available from Nick Ward

THE TADPOLE PRINCE
Everyone's heard of the Frog Prince, now meet the tadpole prince in this
fast-paced and hilarious twist on the traditional fairy tale.
Hardback ISBN 1 84365 016 9 £9.99

And from the Farmer George series

FARMER GEORGE AND THE SNOWSTORM
When poor little Larry gets stuck in the ditch, Farmer George and Sidney
the horse come riding to his rescue through the snowstorm!
Paperback ISBN 1 84365 021 5 £4.99

FARMER GEORGE AND THE LOST CHICK
Farmer George's favourite hen, Clarrie, has lost one of her chicks. All the animals
in the farmyard join in the search, but they can't seem to find him anywhere!
Paperback ISBN 1 86205 432 0 £4.99

FARMER GEORGE AND THE FIELDMICE
It's harvest time on Farmer George's farm and a family of fieldmice realize that his
new combine harvester is heading for their home. Only Tam the dog can save them.
Paperback ISBN 1 86205 413 4 £4.99

FARMER GEORGE AND THE HEDGEHOGS
When Farmer George sets out to clear the yard of leaves, he discovers
that someone else has got there before him…
Paperback ISBN 1 86205 526 2 £4.99

FARMER GEORGE AND THE HUNGRY GUESTS
When food starts mysteriously disappearing from Farmer George's farm,
he and his dog, Tam, go in search of clues to discover the culprits.
Paperback ISBN 1 86205 531 9 £4.99

These books can be ordered direct from Pavilion Children's Books.
Please contact the Marketing Department. But try your bookshop first.